This book belongs to:

While You Were Asleep

By Kedrick T. Lowery

Illustrated by DG

Published by Kedrick T. Lowery

Durham, NC

Library of Congress Control Number: 2020917909

Printed in the United States of America

ISBN-13: 978-0-578-76547-1

DEDICATION

This book is dedicated to our miracle Layla "Grayce" Lowery. May all your dreams come true as you sleep in peace tonight and each night forever.

• • • • •

ACKNOWLEDGEMENTS

Special thanks to my wife and very best friend Dr. Siti Lowery, my niece and bonus daughter Laura Nicole Hairston, my parents Raiford and Arneita Hairston and my Grace Church Family.

CREECH. CREECH. DRIP. DROP. DRIP. DROP. TIC TOCK. TIC TOCK. TIC TOCK.

Layla was preparing for bed and although her mother and father were at her side, all she could do was hear the sounds that were throughout the house.

CREECH. CREECH. DRIP. DROP. DRIP. DROP. TIC TOCK. TIC TOCK. TIC TOCK. TIC TOCK.

Layla had a long day, and so did her mom and dad and it was night-night time.

Each night her parents would come to her room, tuck her in, say a prayer and leave Layla to sleep the night away.

For some reason, this night, all Layla could do was hear the sounds that were throughout the house.

CREECH. CREECH. DRIP. DROP. DRIP. DROP. TIC TOCK. TIC TOCK. TIC TOCK. TIC TOCK.

Layla grabbed her mother and her father's hands. She began to squeeze tightly. "Please don't go!" Layla cried.

Layla you have to go to sleep so that you can get up in time for school tomorrow. *CREECH. CREECH. DRIP. DROP. DRIP. DROP. TIC TOCK. TIC TOCK. TIC TOCK. TIC TOCK.*

Layla's parents noticed there was something different about this night. It was as if Layla was somewhat afraid to let them go.

"Layla, you OK," asked her mom? "Close your eyes and count sheep and you will go to sleep a little faster," said her father.

Layla closed her eyes, she tried to count sheep, but for some reason all Layla could do was hear those sounds.

CREECH. CREECH. DRIP. DROP. DRIP. DROP. TIC TOCK. TIC TOCK. TIC TOCK. TIC TOCK.

Try taking deep breaths. Deep breath in...deep breath out! Deep breath in...deep breath out! This time hold it. Deep breath in.................deep breath out!

Layla took the deep breaths that normally caused her to yawn, but for some reason all Layla could do was hear those sounds.

CREECH. CREECH. DRIP. DROP. DRIP. DROP. TIC TOCK. TIC TOCK. TIC TOCK. TIC TOCK.

Layla squeezed her parents' hands even tighter. Layla's parents looked at each other and realized there was something different about this night. All Layla could do was focus on the sounds she heard throughout the house.

CREECH. CREECH. DRIP. DROP. DRIP. DROP. TIC TOCK. TIC TOCK. TIC TOCK. TIC TOCK. BOOM!

Daddy can you tell me a bedtime story? Layla felt if she could get her parents to stay a little bit longer, she would fall asleep and not have to worry about the sounds she was hearing throughout the house.

CREECH. CREECH. DRIP. DROP. DRIP. DROP. TIC TOCK. TIC TOCK. TIC TOCK. TIC TOCK. BOOM!

Each night, prior to going to sleep, Layla would hear these sounds. The creech, creech of the wind blowing against the window. The **DRIP, DROP, DRIP, DROP** of the water slowly dripping from the sink. The **TIC, TOCK, TICK, TOCK, TICK, TOCK** of the family clock that kept time and the occasional boom of the heater coming on to warm the house.

Layla never told her parents, but she was often frightened by these sounds.

Once again Layla asked, "Daddy can you tell me a bedtime story?" As her mom and dad both yawned, her daddy began to think.

Layla have you ever wondered what happens while you are sleeping?

CREECH. CREECH. DRIP. DROP. DRIP. DROP. TIC TOCK. TIC TOCK. TIC TOCK. TIC TOCK.

No daddy, will you tell me. Her father yawned as he thought of one of his best stories. He shared one his parents shared with him.

Once upon a time, there was a little girl who lived with her parents. Each night they would come to her room, tuck her in, pray with her and then she would sleep the night away.

14

Her day started very early. She would wake up, take her shower, brush her teeth, her mom would comb her hair and then she would get dressed for school.

Before leaving the house to go to her bus stop, she would say a prayer with her parents. Lord thank you for a day filled with blessings. Amen.

Each day this little girl would go to the bus stop. She knew, always look both ways before crossing. She would look to the left and look to the right then she would run as fast as she could across the street going to her bus stop.

This little girl was always taught, when you see people you should speak, so she would speak to all of her friends on the bus stop. "Good morning Kayla." "Hey Cory." Then she would laugh and talk to Natalie.

Each morning when she got on the bus, she would also speak to her bus driver, "Good morning Ms. Tina." The little girl would ride for about fifteen minutes from her bus stop, picking up other students on her way to school and then she would arrive to school.

The little girl loved school. She loved playing with her friends. She loved to talk during breaks. She loved to go outside during recess. She loved lunch. She really loved her teacher. To her school was fun.

After school, the little girl would ride the same bus home. Her mom would meet her at the bus stop and they would walk to the house together. She would eat her favorite snack and then start her homework.

Most days, she would go outside to play with Kayla and Cory after she did her homework. They were her best friends.

After playing outside, the little girl would go home and have dinner with her mom and dad, watch TV and then prepare for bed.

CREECH. CREECH. DRIP. DROP. DRIP. DROP. TIC TOCK. TIC TOCK. TIC TOCK. TIC TOCK. BOOM!

Daddy, those are the sounds I hear before I go to sleep.

These are the sounds the little girl would hear as well. Each night her parents would go to her room, tuck her in, say a prayer and leave her to sleep the night away.

She would fall fast asleep with a big smile on her face while her parents were reading her a bedtime story.

CREECH. CREECH. DRIP. DROP. DRIP. DROP. TIC TOCK. TIC TOCK. TIC TOCK. TIC TOCK. BOOM!

Why was she smiling daddy?

Well Layla, have you ever wondered what happens while you are asleep. What happens daddy?

All night, all day, angels are watching over you. As Layla's dad said the last line of the story, Layla fell soundly asleep!

About the Author

Dr. Kedrick T. Lowery is a Life Coach, Speaker, Author, Marriage and Family Counselor, Mentor, Pastor and most importantly a Husband (of Dr. Siti) and Father (of Layla Grayce and Laura Nicole). Lowery brings over 25 years of education and experiences to his passion for living and helping others live their best life.

Made in the USA
Columbia, SC
06 October 2020